The Way Home

The Way Home

BECKY CITRA

Second Story Press

Library and Archives Canada Cataloguing in Publication

Citra, Becky
The way home / Becky Citra.

Issued also in an electronic format.
ISBN 978-1-927583-01-2

I. Title.

PS8555.I87W39 2013   jC813'.54   C2012-908171-X

Edited by Gena Gorrell
Copyedited by Amanda Thomas
Designed by Melissa Kaita
Cover © iStockphoto

Printed and bound in Canada

Second Story Press gratefully acknowledges the support of the Ontario Arts Council and the Canada Council for the Arts for our publishing program. We acknowledge the financial support of the Government of Canada through the Canada Book Fund.

ONTARIO ARTS COUNCIL
CONSEIL DES ARTS DE L'ONTARIO

Canada Council   Conseil des Arts
for the Arts   du Canada

Published by
Second Story Press
20 Maud Street, Suite 401
Toronto, ON M5V 2M5
www.secondstorypress.ca

To Meghan and her horse, Dylan

CHAPTER ONE

Tory squeezed her legs against the pony's sides. Lucky flicked his ears, but he kept walking. He refused to trot, especially on a scorching day like this.

"You're a lazy pony," said Tory, but she didn't mean it. Lucky was the best thing in her life.

She gave him a gentle kick this time and he trotted for about six steps. Then he settled back to a walk.

It was so hot and so still that Tory thought

she could hear the leaves curling up. The grass was withered and brown and the wildflowers had shriveled.

Everybody was worrying about forest fires. Tory's foster father, Oliver, had taken Lucky's iron shoes off in case they struck a rock and made sparks in the dry grass. He said going barefoot wouldn't hurt the pony.

Tory's foster mother was called Cathy. Tory lived with Oliver and Cathy as part of their family, but she could be moved somewhere else at any time. Her homes and her moves were arranged by Linda, the social worker who was responsible for her.

Tory knew that Oliver and Cathy didn't like her very much. She had heard Cathy say to Linda on the phone, "It's not working out very well. But I told you we would keep her for the summer, and we'll stick to that."

This morning Tory had checked the calendar. She had a little more than three weeks of summer left, before she went to a new foster home. Her stomach churned at the thought. Where would she go? What if her new family didn't like her either? And that meant she had only three more weeks to ride Lucky. She reached forward and patted his thick, snowy mane.

Julia, Oliver and Cathy's daughter, said his mane looked dumb the way it stood up on end, but Tory loved it. Her own long brown hair was just as messy as Lucky's. Sometimes, like today, she tied it back in a ponytail, but usually she let it fly all over the place.

Julia was eleven, two years older than Tory, and her straight blonde hair was always neatly brushed. Julia rode one of the fancy show horses called Barnabas. She was always braiding his silky mane, fastening each braid with a little black elastic band. Tory thought *that* looked dumb but she knew better than to say so.

Oliver was a trainer. He had seven show horses in the barn right now. Some of them belonged to him and Cathy, and some belonged to other people. He worked with the horses every day, getting them ready to compete in horse shows. Tory liked watching him ride the horses in the ring, but she didn't like getting too near. The show horses were much taller than Lucky, and they jumped around a lot and scared her.

Now Tory rode Lucky out of the trees into a wide meadow. This was as far as she was allowed to go. The meadow was called the wetlands, but Tory could see only a little ribbon of sluggish water, far out in a sea of brown grass. Between the grass and the water was a strip of hard, dried-up mud.

Two weeks ago the ground had been alive with hundreds of tiny black frogs, the size of Tory's thumbnail. There were so many that the ground looked as if it were moving, and Tory had been terrified that Lucky would step on them. Cathy said the frogs came every year, and she wasn't sure but she thought they crawled up out of the creek and through the grass.

But today they were gone. Had they dried up in all this heat?

Tory turned Lucky around. He nickered and walked a bit faster.

When they came around the last bend in the trail, Tory cried out loud, "Holy cow!"

In the distance, a huge billow of white cloud sat on top of the hillside. It was smoke from a forest fire and it had been there for a week. But it had grown so much bigger while she was out riding. Staring at the enormous cloud she shivered, and patted Lucky's neck as she rode past the corrals toward the barn.

℧ ℧ ℧

Oliver said the smoke was farther away than it appeared. Miles and miles away, he said. But every day he and Cathy pored over a giant map spread out on the dining-room table. The radio was on all the time, day and night, with news about the fire.

How fast was it moving? Was it coming toward them? Not even Oliver knew for sure.

CHAPTER TWO

Tory took in a deep breath of sweet hay and leather. She loved the way the barn smelled. She took Lucky's saddle and bridle off, brushed his shaggy white coat, and put him in his stall.

Tory had learned how to ride and look after a horse in her first foster home. She had moved into that home when she was four years old because her mother, who was still just a teenager, wasn't able to look after her properly.

For a while Tory's mother had visited her,

but then the visits had stopped and Linda, the social worker, told Tory that her mother had died. Tory had thought she would keep on living with that foster family forever. But when she was eight years old, her foster father got an important new job in Europe, and Tory wasn't allowed to go with them.

She moved again, into her second foster home.

That home didn't work out at all. Tory and the foster mother, Janice, fought all the time. Janice was always blaming Tory for things she hadn't done. When Tory defended herself, Janice said she was lying. After a year, Janice decided that she didn't want to be a foster mother anymore. Right in front of Tory, she told Linda that she couldn't put up with Tory's temper. Blaming Tory again!

Linda told Tory she was sorry about her bad luck. She promised she would find her another family that wanted her. Until then, just for the summer, Tory had to live with Oliver and Cathy.

It made Tory's throat ache to think about all this, so she thought about Lucky instead.

On hot days Oliver and Cathy kept the horses inside the barn, away from the flies. While Tory was brushing Lucky, three heads popped over their stall doors to watch: Julia's bay horse, Barnabas; a gray horse called Destiny; and a chestnut called Orpheus.

The other four stalls were empty. That morning, Oliver had loaded the four horses that belonged in them into the horse trailer. He had taken them to a family called the Mathesons who had a farm far away from the fire. He said he was preparing for a possible evacuation.

Lately Tory had heard the word *evacuation* a lot. People on the radio were talking about it all the time. It meant that if the forest fire came much closer, they would have to grab as many belongings as they could and run to safety.

Tory wasn't too worried. She could pack her few things in her brown duffel bag and backpack in five minutes. She'd done it before. But she couldn't imagine what Julia would do. Julia's purple and white bedroom was crammed with more toys, stuffed animals, books, and clothes than Tory had ever seen in her entire life.

She said good-bye to Lucky and walked to the house. It was the grandest house she had ever lived in. It was built of logs, and the front came up to a high pointed roof and was full of huge windows.

The first day Tory had come here, she had expected to see dogs and cats (didn't all farms have dogs and cats?), but there were none here. When she asked about that, Oliver had frowned and said, "Seven horses are enough to feed and look after." But the truth was that Oliver didn't like dogs. He said they either roamed onto neighbors' farms or barked all night. And Cathy didn't like cats. She didn't like the way they stared.

Tory had known that when Oliver said "seven horses" he was talking about the valuable show horses, but she had muttered, "You mean *eight*." Oliver always forgot about Lucky.

A red truck was parked in front of the house today. It belonged to Mrs. Beeson, Julia's riding teacher. Tory went straight to the kitchen to get a glass of milk. The kitchen was spotless, gleaming with stainless steel, and she was always afraid she would spill something. She took the heavy milk carton out of the fridge, poured her milk carefully, and sat at the table to drink it. The radio on the shelf was turned on and a man was listing all the places that had been put on Evacuation Alert. Oliver had explained that Evacuation Alert meant you had to be ready to go at any time. Their place wasn't on the list – yet.

Julia appeared in the doorway, dressed in snug, stretchy beige pants and tall black riding boots. "Oh, you're here," she said.

Tory wished she had taken her milk to her bedroom, but she didn't think that was allowed. She hated being alone with Julia. She tried to think of something to say. "How was your riding lesson?"

"What?" Julia took a bag of chips out of the cupboard and a can of orange pop from the fridge, two things Tory didn't have the nerve to touch. "Awful. Old Beeswax was in a horrible mood and Barnabas was useless. He wouldn't canter on his left lead at all." When her lesson went badly, Julia always blamed either Mrs. Beeson – who she called Old Beeswax – or Barnabas. Sometimes, like today, she blamed both.

Tory didn't have any idea what a left lead was but she said, "That's too bad."

Julia glared at her and stalked out into the hallway. She came back a second later. "Old Beeswax and Mom are talking about you. In the living room. Do you want to hear what they're saying?"

Tory followed Julia into the hallway. They pressed up against the partly open door that led to the living room.

"She's a wild-looking little thing," said Mrs. Beeson.

"And a temper to match," said Cathy. "She's a poor reader, you know. I tried to help her and she threw the book right across the room."

Mrs. Beeson sighed. "What a shame."

Tory knew what she meant. Mrs. Beeson wasn't sorry that Tory found reading hard. She was sorry that Cathy and Oliver had ever decided to take her.

"We thought she'd be like a sister for Julia," said Cathy. "It was an impulsive idea. Thank goodness it's just for the summer. We're looking forward to having our little family back."

"I don't want a sister," said Julia in Tory's ear.

"I don't want one either," retorted Tory, and she felt her cheeks flame. She *hated* Julia! And except for Lucky, she hated living here! She didn't want to hear any more. She held her head high and marched down the hallway and up the stairs to her little bedroom. She didn't mean to slam the door, it just sort of slammed itself. It sounded awfully loud in the quiet house. Tory was pretty sure Cathy and Mrs. Beeson had heard it.

Oh well, it just gave them one more bad thing to say about her.

CHAPTER THREE

That night, Lucky circled around and around in his stall. He knew something was wrong.

For days now, an acrid smell of smoke had stung his nostrils. It was especially bad when the wind blew over the ridge and down onto the farm. It frightened Lucky, though he didn't understand why.

The other horses were restless too. Barnabas paced in the stall beside Lucky. Destiny whinnied, calling out to the missing horses that

Oliver had taken away that morning. Orpheus took long, slurping gulps of water and blew through his nostrils.

Lucky stopped circling and snatched a mouthful of hay from the hay net hanging in the corner of his stall. He chewed slowly, his ears pricked. Listening.

Wild animals were moving down from the ridge, fleeing the fire and crossing the valley where the farm lay. A cow moose and her baby, a black bear, a family of coyotes. They brought new scents and sounds to Lucky, as they passed through the fields and kept going.

Lucky peered through the metal bars at the top of his stall door. He could see the whites of Destiny's eyes in the stall across from him.

He investigated the steel bar that held his stall door shut. Lucky was a master at opening stall doors, and sometimes Tory forgot to slide the bar all the way across until it latched, the way Oliver had shown her. This was one of those times. He nuzzled the bar and pushed hard. The stall door swung open.

Lucky stepped out into the shadowy aisle. Destiny nickered and he nickered back. Barnabas stopped pacing. Orpheus raised his head from his water, muzzle dripping. They waited to see what Lucky was going to do.

Lucky walked between the stalls, stopping to investigate an empty feed sack and nibbling a few scattered oats. Then he knocked over a metal bucket with a clatter. He skittered in fright on the smooth concrete floor.

At the end of the barn, the big wooden door was propped open to let in a breeze. Lucky stared out at the night. A pale moon made shadows on the ground. For a while, everything was still.

Then Lucky saw two dark shapes step out of a grove of trees. Two deer with long ears and tawny coats. They froze for a moment, watching him with liquid eyes full of curiosity. Then they sprang gracefully over a fence and bounded away into the tall grass.

An uneasy feeling stirred inside Lucky. It told him that something bad was coming. That he should go too. That they should all go. He pawed at the ground, not knowing what to do. He felt torn between the safety of his stall and the urge to run away from the smoke.

Then Destiny whickered softly and Lucky turned back into the barn.

U U U

Tory woke up early in the morning. A hard lump pressed against her elbow. It was the book that Cathy had given her. She had said Tory should finish a chapter every night to help her become a better reader. But the book was boring and full of hard words that Tory couldn't sound out. She had fallen asleep after struggling through two pages.

She shoved the book and it fell on the floor with a thud. She looked around her room gloomily. The bed was crammed into one corner and there was a small dresser with sticky drawers for her clothes. The rest of the room was taken up by a table with a sewing machine on it, and boxes and bags of cloth, sewing patterns, and quilting magazines. A painting of a gray sailboat on a gray sea hung on the wall by the window.

When Cathy had shown Tory her bedroom on Tory's first day, she had apologized. "It's my sewing room," she'd said. "I'll get everything moved out soon. We'll even paint it if you like." Then she'd forgotten all about it.

Suddenly Tory sat up and sniffed. She smelled smoke.

She leapt out of bed and went to the window and peered out. Instead of blue, the sky was pale gray today. A haze hung between the house and the barn.

The forest fire!

She got dressed in record time and hurried downstairs. Oliver and Cathy were huddled in front of the radio. "*Shhh!*" snapped Oliver, although Tory hadn't opened her mouth.

Julia joined them, yawning. She was wearing a pale purple dressing gown and fluffy purple slippers. "What's wrong?"

Oliver turned down the volume on the radio. "We're on the list for Evacuation Alert."

Cathy looked stunned. "We better start packing. Julia, there are boxes in the basement. Get three for yourself."

Julia's face turned scarlet. "Three boxes! There's no way I can put everything in three boxes!"

"That's all we'll have room for," said Cathy firmly. "Tory can help you pack."

"Forget it!" said Julia. "I'll do it myself!"

It took no time at all for Tory to pack her duffel bag. She left it beside her bed and went downstairs to see if there was anything else she could do.

Cathy was wrapping fancy china dishes in newspaper. "These were my grandmother's. I can't leave them behind."

Tory tried to imagine owning something that had belonged to her grandmother. She didn't even know who her grandmother was. "Can I help?"

Cathy frowned. "Why don't you see if Oliver needs you?" Tory guessed that she was thinking about the big blue china platter that Tory had smashed to smithereens the first night she had come. It had been an accident, but Cathy had never let her forget it.

Tory went outside and scanned the sky. The smell of smoke was much stronger than in the house. She looked to see what had happened to the great cloud of smoke on the hillside, but it had disappeared in the haze.

Oliver didn't want her help either. He had just finished hooking the horse trailer to the truck. He told Tory that they would have to leave all the saddles and bridles behind, but that he was going to pack up the trophies and ribbons.

"Maybe Cathy can use you," he said.

Tory sighed. She went into the barn to visit Lucky. All the horses were restless, shifting back and forth in their stalls and nervously snatching mouthfuls of hay. She thought Lucky's dark eyes looked especially worried.

"It's okay," she said. "Oliver's going to take you to a new home. Just for a little while. Then you'll come back here."

After all, Oliver said the fire was still miles away. The Evacuation Alert was just in case.

Nobody stopped for lunch. Boxes piled up on the front porch. Tory and Julia helped carry the lighter ones out to the truck and car.

In the early afternoon, a man in a red pickup truck with writing on the side roared down the gravel driveway. He jumped out, holding a clipboard in his hand.

"The fire is near the top of the ridge," he

shouted. "You've got to get out of here! One hour max!"

Julia burst into tears. Tory knew she should feel sorry for her but she didn't. She felt oddly excited, as if something big was about to change in her life.

"Bring out the last few things," said Oliver. "Then we'll load the horses."

CHAPTER FOUR

Barnabas went first, clattering up the ramp into the back of the horse trailer. He whinnied loudly and tossed his head. Destiny didn't want to follow him. She braced her feet on the ground. Oliver tapped her with a whip and she lunged inside. Orpheus pranced all the way from his stall to the trailer and Oliver kept saying, "Whoa, boy. Easy boy."

Tory was afraid of the big show horses and she stayed well back. "Lucky, don't forget Lucky," she whispered to herself.

Lucky swung his head around in fright when he came out of the barn. Tory could see the whites of his eyes. "Cathy, give me a hand here," said Oliver.

"Lucky hates going into the trailer," said Julia to Tory.

Cathy held Lucky's lead rope and Oliver walked behind with the whip. Tory held her breath.

At the last minute, the pony planted his feet. Oliver tapped him with the whip. Again, harder. Lucky reared up.

"Bad horse!" said Oliver.

Cathy led Lucky in a tight circle and back to the ramp. Oliver hit him hard with the whip. Lucky skittered sideways and whinnied, and his hooves clattered on the hard ground.

Cathy circled him again and again. Each time, Lucky refused to go into the trailer. Tory's heart pounded.

"This is the last time," grunted Oliver.

Lucky backed up, and Oliver slashed the whip across his rear legs. It made a horrible smacking sound. Tory closed her eyes. She wished she could close her ears too.

"It's no use," said Oliver finally. His forehead was wet with sweat.

"We can't leave him here," said Cathy.

"Oh yes we can. I'll open the gate in the corral and the gate in the bottom field so he won't be trapped. There's nothing else we can do. We've run out of time."

Tory thought she was going to be sick. The gate in the bottom field was set in the middle of a wire fence, where the farm ended. On the other side were acres and acres of wilderness. Wild animals lived out there, wolves and bears and cougars.

Oliver let Lucky loose in the corral. The pony raced up and down along the fence, churning up clouds of dust.

"Why don't you get going?" said Oliver to

Cathy. "I'll bring the girls in the truck. I'll open those gates and then we'll be right behind you."

Cathy drove off in the car. Julia climbed into the front seat of the truck and Tory squished into the back, beside a big box. She turned her head to look out the window. Tears blurred her eyes.

Too soon, Oliver was back. The last thing Tory heard as they drove away was Lucky's frantic whinny.

CHAPTER FIVE

Lucky watched Oliver climb into the truck and slam the door. He galloped up and down the corral fence, whinnying. He didn't want to be left alone.

As the back of the horse trailer disappeared around a bend in the driveway, Lucky heard one of the horses calling to him. Then everything was silent.

Lucky had seen the horse trailer take horses away before. But three or four horses had always stayed home with him. He had never been left all by himself.

After a long time, he stopped running. His sides heaved in and out. His neck was slick with sweat. He stood very still, his ears pricked forward, and watched the bend in the driveway, waiting for someone to come back.

But no one did.

With a grunt, the pony flopped down on his side and rolled and rolled in the dirt. He wanted to get the sweat out of his coat and the smell of smoke out of his nostrils. Then he stood up and gave a great shake, making a huge cloud of dust. He could still smell the smoke. It burned his eyes and made it hard to breathe.

Lucky took a long drink from the old bathtub that Oliver had left full of water. For a second he thought he heard the sound of the truck. He stood still, water dripping from his muzzle. Then he sighed and took another drink. He pushed some hay around with his nose, but he didn't feel hungry.

For a long time, he stood by the corral fence and watched the driveway. The smoke became thicker. In the distance, on top of the hillside, red and orange flames glowed against the sky.

Lucky waited and waited.

No one came.

U U U

In the truck, Julia peppered her father with questions. "Are we going to Springton? Can we stay overnight in a hotel? What if the fire gets that far?"

"The fire is nowhere near Springton," Oliver said confidently. "And we're going to stay with the Mathesons. The other horses are already there."

Tory had never been to the Mathesons' house but she knew they lived a little ways past the other side of Springton. The daughter, Deanna, was one of Julia's friends. Julia talked about her all the time.

Springton was an hour's drive away. Tory sometimes went there with Cathy to get groceries.

Usually they stopped to see Linda, the social worker, who had an office in the town. One time, Cathy drove Tory past the brown house where Tory had lived with her last foster family. Tory stared out the window at the slide and swing set in the front yard, remembering all the times she had played there.

Oliver turned off the rough farm road onto a smooth highway. After a few minutes, he stopped at the small general store, where he and Cathy got their mail and odds and ends like milk and bread. Pickup trucks and vans packed with belongings were lined up at the gas pump. People stood around in small groups, talking.

Oliver waited his turn for gas and then went inside the store to pay. When he came back out he said, "They're closing up in a couple of hours. They're leaving too. Just to be on the safe side."

He flipped on the radio and they listened to reports about the fire for the rest of the way. It was hot, but the windows in the truck were shut to keep the smoke out. A trickle of sweat crawled down Tory's back.

The radio announcer interviewed some of the families fleeing the fire. Then a man from the forestry department said, "Fifty more firefighters and three water bombers are expected in the next few hours."

"Thank goodness," sighed Oliver.

Oliver made one more stop when they got to Springton, at the community center. Cathy pulled up beside him in the car. Oliver checked on the horses in the trailer while Cathy and the girls went inside. The room was packed with people and there was a buzz of voices, some worried, some excited. Tables were set up with coffee and boxes of donuts. Volunteers at other tables were writing down the names of all the people who had been evacuated. It was like a party.

For a few seconds, Tory forgot about Lucky. While Cathy registered their names, Tory helped herself to a donut covered with chocolate icing and red and yellow sprinkles. But as soon as she took one bite, she felt her tummy tighten. She couldn't swallow. She wrapped the donut in a napkin and left it on the edge of a table.

Tory followed Cathy and Julia back out to the truck. She slumped against the window and blinked back sudden tears. What was going to happen to Lucky? Would she ever see him again?

CHAPTER SIX

"This is Tory," said Julia. "She's the foster kid I told you about. She's staying with us for the summer."

Deanna Matheson stared at Tory, her mouth hanging open. When they had arrived at the Mathesons' farm, Tory had followed Julia out to the barn, where they found Deanna leaning over a stall door and talking to a tall black horse. Deanna had shrieked when she saw Julia. Now they had their arms wrapped around each other.

"What grade are you going into?" asked Deanna.

"Four," said Tory.

"Liar! said Julia.

Tory's cheeks flamed. Julia should mind her own business.

"You don't look old enough for fourth grade," said Deanna bluntly.

"Well, I am." That part was true. Tory was nine and she was *supposed* to be going into grade four.

"She can hardly read, so she has to do grade three over again," said Julia.

"Shut up," muttered Tory.

After that, Deanna lost interest in Tory. Tory sat on a hay bale and half-listened while the girls talked about Julia's horse, Barnabas, and Deanna's horse, the black one in the stall, called Prince. They made plans to ride as soon as Barnabas settled down. Oliver had put all their horses in one big field and Tory could hear them whinnying and galloping around.

"I was just about to groom Prince," said Deanna. "I'm trying to get him in perfect condition for next week's show."

"I'll help," said Julia quickly. "You stay here, Tory."

Tory shrugged.

"She's afraid of real horses," said Julia. "She'll only ride Lucky, that old pony."

"I'm not afraid!" said Tory hotly. She stood up.

"Okay then, you can brush Prince's tail." Julia glanced sideways at Deanna and grinned.

Tory tried to swallow her fear while Deanna brought the big horse out of his stall and fastened him in crossties. Deanna gave her a stiff plastic currycomb. Tory eyed Prince warily. He seemed calm, though his ears flicked back and forth every time one of the horses outside whinnied. She edged up to his hind end and picked up part of his tail.

It wasn't too bad. The comb ran through the hair easily because there were no tangles, and

Tory started to relax. Julia was brushing Prince's neck and Deanna was rummaging around in a plastic bin, muttering about hoof polish. "Where is Lucky, anyway?" she said over her shoulder. "I didn't see him."

"We didn't bring him," said Julia.

Tory stiffened.

"He wouldn't load in the trailer." Just for a second, Julia looked worried. "But it's not like he's trapped or anything. Dad opened the gates." She added coolly, "It's his own fault. You know how dumb he can be."

A red-hot sliver of anger flashed through Tory. How *dare* Julia say that about Lucky! Without thinking, she hurled the currycomb at Julia's face.

Julia screamed.

For a second, Tory felt immense satisfaction at the smacking sound the comb made. Then she felt frightened by what she had done. There was a red patch on Julia's cheek, and tiny pinpoints of blood.

"I'm telling!" Julia spat out the words and fled from the barn.

"Now you've done it," said Deanna. She put Prince back in his stall. Then she was gone too.

Tory sank back on the hay bale and waited. She was in major trouble now.

It didn't take Oliver long to come. His face was grim as he towered above her. "I'm disappointed in you. *Very* disappointed. What were you thinking? You could have poked Julia's eye out."

It would have served her right, thought Tory. But it was no use telling Oliver that. Everyone always blamed her.

Oliver kept on. "You're nine years old. You should know better."

Tory wished she could drown out Oliver's words. She hummed inside her head.

"What do you have to say for yourself?"

This time, Tory let the hum escape so Oliver heard. His lips tightened in a line. She pressed her lips together too, and hummed louder.

Oliver sighed. "I think you need a timeout. I want you to go and sit in the truck for an hour."

Tory didn't care that timeouts were for babies. She *wanted* to sit in the truck. Then she wouldn't have to see nasty Julia or her stupid friend Deanna. Instead, she could think about Lucky.

∪ ∪ ∪

Cathy came out to the truck and told Tory it was time for supper, but Tory refused to get out. She waited until it was dark before she ventured inside the house. The adults were in the living room, listening to more fire news on the TV. She hesitated in the doorway.

Cathy looked up. "The girls are in Deanna's room. We've put a sleeping bag and a mat in there for you."

Tory's stomach rumbled, but Cathy said nothing about supper. Then Deanna's mother,

Martha, said, "Go into the kitchen and help your-self to a big bowl of cereal, Tory. And a banana if you like."

It took Tory a few minutes to find every-thing. As she ate her cornflakes, she decided that Martha was nicer than Cathy. She chewed slowly, imagining the Mathesons as her next fos-ter family. She sighed.

She remembered to rinse her bowl and spoon and then went in search of Deanna's bedroom.

Julia and Deanna were lying on Deanna's double bed, in their pajamas, looking at maga-zines. Trying not to stare, Tory checked out Julia's cheek. There was still a faint red mark. *Good!*

Tory changed into her pajamas in the bath-room. She crawled into her sleeping bag on the floor and closed her eyes tight. She heard Julia whisper something and then Deanna giggled. They were probably talking about her.

Tory scrunched deeper into her sleeping bag. She fell asleep worrying about Lucky.

CHAPTER SEVEN

By early evening, Lucky had drunk most of the water. He had paced around and around the corral hundreds of times. He knew that the gate was open.

He also knew that it was time to go.

As he trotted through the open gate, he had only one thought: *Get away from the smoke!* Something told him to hurry, so he kept trotting through a field of tall brown grass that was so dry and brittle it scratched his legs.

An eagle soared high above him, its white head gleaming. A mouse burrowed into the grass to get out of the way. No one else saw Lucky go by.

At the bottom of the field, he crossed a creek bed that had dried up to a trickle. His hooves churned the last of the water to mud. When he scrambled up the far bank, he found another open gate, this one in the middle of a wire fence. On the other side of the fence was a thick pine and spruce forest. He gave one last lonely whinny, but no one answered him. He trotted through the gate into the forest.

Lucky followed a rough, grassy road with two ruts made by the tires of Oliver's ATV. The road went deep into the forest. Dead grass rustled against his legs; twigs snapped under his hooves.

The road ended in a clearing where Oliver cut up dead trees for firewood. Lucky stood still for a moment, thinking about what to do.

A Great Gray Owl swooped by on muffled wings. A squirrel chattered from the branch of a pine tree. In a small way they were company for Lucky, who felt very alone. He whinnied once, a shrill cry calling desperately to the other horses. When there was no answer, he left the clearing and set off on a narrow deer trail.

Away from the smoke – that was the rule that guided the pony, but the smoke followed him, burning his eyes and making it hard to breathe.

As the night shadows deepened, the trees closed in. The trail was so narrow that branches slapped against his sides and pine needles caught in his mane. He had never been in this forest before. Every one of his senses was alert to danger. His ears were pricked and his nostrils flared. His eyes searched the darkness.

But he was exhausted from his frantic day of racing back and forth in the corral, so he didn't notice the first gray shape that slipped along beside him through the trees. In a few minutes it was joined by another, and then two more.

Four timber wolves – cruising through the forest, empty stomachs grumbling, cranky from the smoke and the heat. Four pairs of golden eyes glowing in the night.

Lucky sensed something now. He broke into an anxious trot.

The wolves separated, two on either side of Lucky. They loped along easily, gliding in and out of the trees, keeping pace. There was no need now to stay hidden. They were hungry, but they were in no hurry. They could go a long way on their lean, strong legs.

Lucky stumbled, tumbling almost onto his knees. He scrabbled upright, his eyes rolling in fear.

Run!

He plunged ahead, the trail lost, his only thought to escape the wolves.

Run!

Suddenly he was startled by a newcomer, a young deer that bolted in front of him. It bounded through the trees, terrified, as it picked up the scent of the wolves.

The four timber wolves – their hunger growing – were distracted by the thought of easier prey. They veered after the deer and chased it down the side of a steep gully.

Lucky kept running, his chest tight and his legs aching. He crashed through bushes and dodged trees until his sides heaved and dots of foam flecked his sweat-darkened neck. He ran until he could run no more.

Then he stood, head hanging.

Night closed in around the abandoned pony. He was worn out. He desperately needed water. And he had no idea where he was or where to go.

CHAPTER EIGHT

"Don't forget to include Tory," said Deanna's mother, Martha.

It was morning and Tory was in the kitchen, still finishing her toast. Martha was talking to Julia and Deanna in the living room. She didn't know that Tory could hear.

Tory stopped chewing so she could hear even better.

"We were going to go riding," said Julia. "There's nothing here that she can ride."

That made Tory think of Lucky again. A lump formed in her throat and she put her toast down. She couldn't eat another bite.

"After your ride, then. How about taking a board game out to the deck?"

"I tried playing Monopoly with her at home," complained Julia. "She picked up the board and tipped it over when she was losing."

"*After* you cheated," Tory muttered under her breath. Julia, who had been the banker, had thought Tory was so stupid that she wouldn't notice when Julia gave her the wrong money. And why did Martha think that Tory wanted to play with Julia and Deanna anyway?

She threw the rest of her toast in the garbage and then stomped outside through the back door. The sky was blue and there wasn't a hint of smoke in the air. It was hard to believe that a forest fire was raging not that far away. She supposed it had something to do with the wind, because Deanna's dad said that a few days ago they had had a lot of smoke.

Everyone was hoping rain would come and put out the fire, but Tory couldn't see one single cloud. And it was hot already, though it was only nine o'clock. The day stretched ahead.

She watched from the back step while Julia and Deanna walked over to the barn in their riding clothes. A black Lab with runny eyes lay down beside her and she patted him gently. Deanna had a tabby cat, too; Tory had found him curled up on the end of her sleeping bag when she woke up. She spotted him now, crouching in the tall grass beside a fence.

Tory wished again that Cathy and Oliver had some pets. Not that it really mattered. The summer would be over soon and she would be leaving. Linda still hadn't told her where she would be going. Sometimes she felt like throwing up when she thought about moving to a new family. Would they like her? Would they want her? Or would they just send her on to some other family?

In a little while Martha came outside. "How would you like to go to town with me?"

There was nothing else to do. "Okay," said Tory.

Going to Springton with Martha was a lot different from going with Cathy, who always had a list, and hurried from store to store with no time to really look at anything.

Martha let Tory take five minutes deciding what kind of cookies to buy. At the drugstore, Tory looked at all the stuffed animals. At the tack store, she admired the saddles and colored halters and decided which one would look best on Lucky.

Then they went to Dairy Queen and Tory got fries *and* a Blizzard.

As she slurped up her Blizzard, she examined her idea about the Mathesons being her next foster family. Martha liked her, she could tell. And there was plenty of room to bring Lucky. That is, if Oliver and Cathy let her. They probably would. She had heard Oliver complain lots of times that since Julia had outgrown Lucky, they really didn't need him anymore.

Thinking of Lucky made Tory bite down hard on her lip. She decided instead to think about the news that Deanna's father had announced at breakfast. "They're containing the fire. They've got extra fire crews working. They're going to keep it out of the valley."

"Our beautiful house," Cathy had cried thankfully. "Maybe we can go home soon."

Martha had turned to Tory. "That old Lucky will be waiting for you when you get back, Tory. You wait and see."

In the afternoon, while Julia read, Deanna showed Tory how to play one of her games on the computer. She gave Tory a super-long turn. She was a lot nicer when you got her away from Julia.

By bedtime, Tory had convinced herself that it was going to happen. The Mathesons really would let her come and be their new daughter. The only bad thing would be that Julia would come to visit sometimes, but Tory could pretend to be busy on those days.

Just before she brushed her teeth, she slipped down to the kitchen for a glass of milk. She stopped at the doorway. Cathy and Martha were sitting at the table with mugs of tea.

"I can't imagine why you decided to take a foster child," said Martha. "Tory seems like such a needy little girl."

"We mostly did it as a favor," said Cathy. "Linda Jenson, her social worker, is a friend of mine. And it's just until they can find her a more permanent home."

"Well," said Martha, "it's a lot of responsibility, taking on a foster child. You just don't know what kind of problems you're getting into." She added firmly, "We would *never* take that risk."

Tears stung Tory's eyes. She crept off to bed.

CHAPTER NINE

A strong wind blew into Lucky's face, keeping the smoke away. A bright full moon lit up the forest.

He had walked most of the day, resting occasionally in the shade under the tall pine trees. Sometimes he followed deer and bear trails and sometimes he made his own way. When he was hungry, he tore off long pieces of dry grass and slowly chewed them. He longed for fresh grass or the sweet hay that he was fed at the farm. But even more than that, he longed for water.

He passed by two small swamps that looked like grassy islands in the middle of the forest. He investigated each one hopefully, stepping cautiously through bulrushes and reeds. His hooves made big holes in the soft, spongy ground, but the water had dried up weeks ago.

Just after midnight, Lucky came to an old fence made out of wooden rails. Many of the rails were broken. In places, the fence had collapsed into the ground. He stepped through one of these openings and kept going. A few minutes later, he stood at the edge of a field. On the other side, a silver roof glinted in the moonlight.

Lucky knew that he was near people again. And people meant water. He nickered and his hooves quickened as he made his way across the field. He stepped over another broken piece of fence and stopped at the edge of a weed-choked yard.

In the middle of the yard was a white trailer. On one end of the trailer sagged a wooden lean-to with a piece of blue tarp for a roof. There were no curtains at the trailer windows, which looked black and empty.

The yard was littered with pieces of old machinery and other junk – a rusty tractor, a car with broken windows, a washing machine, a fridge with a smashed door. Nettles grew right up through the middle of a pile of worn-out tires.

Lucky waited for a few minutes, his ears pricked. Nothing. A gust of wind tore at the edge of the blue tarp, which flapped and fluttered with a rattling sound. He jumped back, his muscles bunched, ready to run.

He sensed that this was a bad place to be, but his thirst drove him forward across the yard. He poked around the front of the trailer for a few minutes. A plastic bag containing tin cans, potato peelings, and a piece of rotten steak had been torn open. Its contents were strewn everywhere. He nosed the garbage, but found nothing of interest. He ventured around the back. More nettles grew here, and there was a small tumble-down shelter with two stalls.

One of the stall doors was open. He advanced cautiously, his nostrils searching for the scent of water. He stuck his head through the doorway. It was too dark inside to see anything, but a musty smell of moldy hay greeted him.

No water.

He took a few steps farther and banged his hoof against a feed bucket. It tipped over with a clatter. Startled, he backed out of the shelter.

Clouds scudded across the sky, blocking out the moon. Lucky couldn't see anything now. He didn't like being by himself. He whinnied loudly, again and again, desperate for someone to come. But no window opened at the trailer. No one peered out the door to see what was causing the commotion. The only sound was the flapping blue tarp.

Lucky picked his way through a patch of tall

weeds that grew beside the shelter. He had made up his mind to return to the forest.

Suddenly, something razor-sharp bit into his front legs.

Frightened, he tried to plunge forward, but something pulled him back. It was as if a hundred sharp teeth were hanging onto him, ripping his skin. He tried leaping sideways but the pain was worse, like nothing he had ever felt before. He kicked out, frantic to escape. Whatever this terrifying thing was, it tightened around his front legs, binding his feet together.

And then Lucky couldn't move at all.

CHAPTER TEN

Rain!

It woke Tory in the morning, rattling like pebbles at the window in Deanna's bedroom. She slipped out of her sleeping bag and hurried downstairs.

Cathy was sitting on a sofa in the living room, curled up in a blanket with a mug of cocoa.

"It's raining!" said Tory.

"I know," said Cathy. "I've been up for hours,

listening to it. I just had the radio on. We can go home today."

Not *my* home, thought Tory. But she was too excited to worry about that. She took a deep breath. "Do you think Lucky will still be there?"

Cathy hesitated. "I think he'll be close by. He probably never even left. After all, the fire never reached our valley."

Tory held onto that thought all morning. Lucky was safe. He *had* to be. Breakfast took forever. Now that the danger had passed, no one was in a hurry to do anything. Tory worried that they would have to pack up all the boxes that had been stored in the Mathesons' garage and put them in the car and truck. It would take ages. To her great relief, Oliver and Cathy decided to come back for their belongings when it wasn't raining.

Finally Oliver and Deanna's dad ventured outside to load four of the horses into the horse trailer – Barnabas, Destiny, Orpheus, and a black horse called Jet. Oliver would get the others when he returned for the boxes. Tory watched through the rain-streaked window, whispering at them to hurry.

She thought Oliver and Cathy would never finish saying their thank-yous and good-byes, but at last they were on their way. This time, Julia and Tory rode in the car with Cathy. The windshield wipers swished back and forth. Julia, who had spent half the night whispering with Deanna in her double bed, leaned against the window and fell asleep.

How *could* she sleep? Didn't she care about Lucky? Tory sat bolt upright. Her stomach was in a knot as a hundred questions tumbled around in her head. Was Lucky hungry? He must have eaten all his hay by now. Did he have enough water? Oliver had left the bathtub in the corral full but how much did a pony drink? She hoped Lucky had gone into the shelter to get out of the rain.

Cathy had to make one stop in Springton, at the bank. The next stop was the general store near their farm, where she ran in to pick up the mail. Tory bounced on the seat impatiently. She thought she would burst by the time Cathy turned onto the farm road.

Oliver was there ahead of them. He had put on a rain slicker and was unloading the last horse from the trailer. Tory practically fell out of the car. "For heavens sake, Tory, wait until I've stopped!" snapped Cathy.

Tory ran to the corral fence. The shelter at the far end was empty. Some hay was scattered around and the bathtub still had water in it. But there was no sign of the white pony.

A tight feeling squeezed her chest. "Lucky!" she yelled. "*Lucky!*"

"Come inside, Tory," called Cathy. "You're going to get soaked." She and Julia dashed through the rain to the house. Oliver walked over to the corral where Tory still stood, rain mixing with the tears on her cheeks. He frowned. "He won't be far. You'd better come in now. We'll look for him when the rain lets up." He put his hand on her arm.

Tory wrenched herself away. Oliver didn't care. *Nobody* cared except her. She made up her mind fast. She scrambled over the fence, and ran across the corral and through the gate that Oliver had left open for Lucky. She could hear Oliver shouting something at her, but she kept running.

Down through the field she raced, the wet grass slapping at her jeans. Wind drove the stinging rain into her face. She crossed the creek bed at the bottom of the field, mud squelching up over her runners.

She stopped at the open gate in the middle of the wire fence. Her heart beating fast, she stared into the dripping forest. It was dark in there, almost as dark as night, and the trees swayed and groaned in the wind.

"Lucky!" she shouted. "Lucky!" The rain plastered her hair to her head. Her drenched sweatshirt clung to her back like clammy skin. But she didn't want to go back to the house. She would *never* go back until she found Lucky.

Tory took a deep breath. She took a few hesitant steps forward, through the open gate, and she started to run.

CHAPTER ELEVEN

Lucky shivered. At first his thick white coat had shed the rain. Now, by the middle of the day, he was wet right down to his skin. He was stiff from standing in one place for so long. He was hungry. And he was terribly thirsty.

In the morning light he had seen what was trapping him – a coil of jagged barbed wire. It had been left to rust in the tall weeds and it was now wrapped tightly around his front legs. There was no way he could work himself free.

So he just stood there.

Finally he heard something. He swiveled his ears toward the sound of a truck rattling over a gravel road. A few moments later, he heard a door slam at the front of the white trailer. And then nothing.

He cried out – a loud, shrill whinny, begging for help.

A man in a dark gray oilskin coat appeared at the side of the trailer. He stared in Lucky's direction.

Lucky whinnied again.

"Hey! Where did you come from?"

The man waded through the weeds and stood beside Lucky. He was tall and heavy, with a black beard and a sour smell. He stared at the pony with small bloodshot eyes. "You got yourself in a mess."

Lucky trembled. He was afraid of the man's smell and his rough voice.

The man muttered, "I'll have to get my fencing

pliers." He grinned suddenly, his mouth full of blackened teeth. "Don't go anywhere."

He disappeared around the trailer, but he was back in a few minutes with a halter and a rope and a pair of pliers. He slid the halter over Lucky's head. "Ain't taking any chances on you getting away. You're a good-looking pony. Someone will be looking for you, and that might mean a reward."

He bent down, puffing and grunting, and cut the wire away from Lucky's legs. When Lucky was free, his instinct told him to run, but the man held him tight with the rope.

"We'll just put you in here," he said, leading Lucky to the old shelter. Lucky limped, the numbness in his legs turning quickly to pain. The man yanked roughly on the rope, jerking the pony's head.

When Lucky was safely in one of the stalls, the man took off the rope and halter. He kicked forward some of the moldy hay that was piled up in the corner. "You can eat this," he growled. He shut the bottom half of the stall door, slid the latch across, and leaned on the door to study Lucky. "Just maybe my luck's changing," he said. "I bet there'll be a nice fat reward for you. I ain't going to give you back for nothing, that's for sure."

Lucky backed into a corner of the stall.

"After all," said the man, "if I hadn't come back when I did, you'd have died. You could say I saved your life."

The man left Lucky and walked back to the trailer. He planned to go to the store in the morning and ask around to see if anyone was missing a pony. But he wouldn't admit that he had the pony. Not yet. He'd give the owner time to get a whole lot more worried.

It had been a few years since the man had looked after animals – a pair of goats, some pigs, and a thin, half-starved dog. He didn't know that Lucky was desperate for water. He didn't know that the wounds from the barbed wire would become horribly infected if they weren't looked after.

He also didn't know that Lucky was a master at opening stall doors.

CHAPTER TWELVE

Tory ran along the rough road into the forest, stumbling over the ruts and bumps. After a few minutes she slowed to a walk, sucking in gulps of air, trying to stop shivering. Rain slithered down her neck and her runners were soaking wet.

"Lucky!" she screamed. "Lucky!"

She peered into the dark trees, afraid of what the forest might hold. *Don't think about bears and cougars*, she told herself. *Don't.*

It was hard to keep going. But Lucky was

out there somewhere and he needed her. She was certain of that.

A faint roar behind her made her spin around. The roar grew louder, and Oliver appeared around a bend in the track, hunched over the seat of the ATV, squinting from under the hood of a flapping rain slicker. Tory felt weak with relief at not being alone. But she was afraid that Oliver would be angry.

He wasn't. He had a rain slicker for her, which she slithered into, and he told her to climb up behind him. She had ridden only once before on the ATV. She had loved it. But this time she was too worried about Lucky to enjoy herself.

Oliver shouted so Tory could hear him over the roar of the engine. "The rain's probably washed away Lucky's tracks, but keep your eyes peeled just in case." He drove slowly along the rough road. When he got to the woodcutting clearing, he stopped and turned off the ATV's motor. Tory hopped off.

"That's as far as we can go on this thing," he said. "We'll walk for a bit, see if we can spot anything."

The rain had eased to a drizzle but the trees were still dripping. When Tory brushed against branches, water drops sprinkled her face.

She followed Oliver along a narrow deer trail. Once, he stopped and said, "These branches here that are broken? That could be from Lucky." Then he stopped walking and frowned. He was staring at something on the ground.

"What is it?" said Tory, her heart beating fast.

"Scat." *Scat* was the fancy word for *poop*, Tory knew.

"Wolf scat. Lots of it. There must have been more than one wolf come this way. Three or four maybe."

Wolves! Her stomach lurched.

"The scat could have been here for a week or even longer," he added quickly. "It's impossible to tell with all the rain."

They walked for another twenty minutes, to the edge of a steep gully. Oliver turned to Tory. "There's not much point going any farther. We'll never find Lucky out here. He's probably made his way to a farm somewhere. You'll see, he'll turn up snug and warm in someone's barn."

All the way back, Tory told herself over and over again that Oliver was right. Lucky was safe.

But prickles ran up and down her spine. Wolves!

ᑌ ᑌ ᑌ

The man was finishing his sixth can of beer when he thought about water for Lucky.

"Don't want that pony dying on me," he mumbled. "Not with all that reward money I could get."

He heaved himself off the couch with a grunt and took a pail out to the pump in the yard.

He filled it with brownish water and carried it to the shelter.

"Hey!" he cried. "How did that happen?"

The stall door was open and the pony was gone.

CHAPTER THIRTEEN

After dinner, Cathy phoned all their neighbors, asking if anyone had seen Lucky. No one had, but everyone promised to call back if they had any news.

Tory asked Cathy for paper and felt pens. "I'm going to make a sign about Lucky to put up at the store."

"Great idea. Make a few. Oliver's going back to the Mathesons' place tomorrow to get the horses, and he could put some up in town."

Tory sat at the kitchen table and thought hard about what to write. Her first attempt was terrible, her printing crooked and the letters growing smaller and smaller as they advanced across the paper. Fiercely she crumpled it into a ball.

Cathy, who was unloading the dishwasher, looked as if she was going to say something, then changed her mind. Tory scrunched up her second attempt too. She smashed the felt pen on the table and flung her head down on her arms. Everything she did was messed up. Tears burned behind her eyelids.

Cathy leaned over her. For a second, Tory thought she was going to hug her, and she tensed. But Cathy never hugged. Instead, she took a fresh piece of paper and drew some faint pencil lines. "That'll keep your letters straight."

The lines helped. Tory ended up making five signs, each with the word REWARD in bold red capital letters at the top. Cathy showed her how to make a row of telephone numbers at the bottom, and to cut little slits so that someone could tear off a number.

Oliver came in. He raised his eyebrows when he saw the word REWARD but he promised to take the signs with him in the morning.

That evening, Tory couldn't keep her eyes open, and Cathy sent her to bed early. She was just drifting off to sleep when her bedroom door opened.

Julia stood in the crack of light from the hall. "Hey, Tory. I just...um, wanted to say I'm sorry Lucky's missing."

Tory pretended to be asleep. Confusing thoughts swirled in her head. Oliver and Cathy had been nice to her today. And now Julia.

She waited until Julia left, then rolled over on her stomach and pressed her face into her pillow. Things were easier when she could hate everybody.

∪ ∪ ∪

The night sky was clear and the air was washed clean after the rain. The smoke was gone. Lucky had a new rule to guide him now – get as far away as possible from the man with the rough voice and the sour smell.

He had left the valley bottom late that afternoon and started to climb the mountain. Every step had hurt. The dried blood had caked on his front legs, and the skin around the wounds was puffy and burning.

The sound of rushing water had spurred him on. Above him a stream, swollen by the heavy rains, tumbled down between boulders. He lowered his head and took a long, soothing drink. He rested for a while, water dripping from his muzzle, then he took another drink and continued to climb up the mountain.

Now he was resting. All around him, the air was full of animal sounds – tiny feet scurrying, leaves rustling, twigs cracking. Around midnight a cougar passed close by, curious about the horse but not a threat. Lucky dozed, too tired and sore to care.

In the morning, Lucky's legs felt as if they were on fire. He ate some grass and found a small spring for water. Then he continued climbing, until he was on top of the mountain.

Below him stretched a new valley, long and narrow, with golden meadows and groves of trees. A silver river, glimmering in the sun, wound like a ribbon down the middle.

Lucky ventured down the slope, his hooves skidding on the rough ground. He was hobbling badly now, and he kept his head low to the ground to avoid stumbling. When he finally reached the floor of the valley, his nostrils quivered. He could smell the cool, clean scent of the river.

He limped across a meadow, snatching a mouthful of grass now and then, until he reached the low, gravelly bank of the river. He waded out to his knees.

A sudden movement caught his eye. It was a boy, a little way down from him. He was sitting on a boulder, hurling rocks into the water. A small dog nosed around the rocks beside him. The boy stood up and walked along the bank until he was opposite the strange pony that had appeared out of nowhere.

He was a thin boy with brown hair that flopped over his forehead. He was wearing baggy shorts and was barefoot. He pushed his hair back and stared at Lucky.

Lucky stared back. He thought about running away, but the icy water felt wonderful on his burning legs. So he stayed where he was.

The dog ran up and down the shore, barking, as the boy plunged into the river and waded toward Lucky.

CHAPTER FOURTEEN

Early the next morning, Oliver took Tory's signs with him. The phone rang four times before eleven o'clock and Tory jumped every time. She hung by Cathy's shoulder until she knew the call wasn't about Lucky. The last time it was Linda, the social worker, and Cathy shut the kitchen door so Tory couldn't hear.

"It's too soon for someone to phone," said Julia scornfully. "What do you expect – someone's going to see your sign as soon as Dad puts it up?"

79

She seemed to have forgotten that she had felt sorry for Tory the night before. Tory wondered if she had imagined Julia coming to her room. And Cathy was cranky, shooing Tory outside with the promise that she would call her right away if there was any news.

When Tory came back inside at lunchtime, Julia had propped a book up against the sugar bowl and was reading. Tory ate her tuna fish sandwich in silence. She swung her legs and by accident kicked Julia.

"Hey!" said Julia. "What was that for?" She kicked Tory back, hard.

"Ow!" yelped Tory. She leaned forward and knocked over Julia's milk so that it poured onto her lap.

"You idiot! These are my best shorts!" shrieked Julia. "Now they're ruined."

Cathy sent both of them to their rooms. Julia slammed her door but Tory's anger had drained away. She lay on her bed, listening for the phone.

She told herself that if she hoped hard enough, someone would phone to say they had found Lucky.

But no one did.

ᘮ ᘮ ᘮ

The boy waded deeper into the river, approaching Lucky slowly. When he was close enough to touch the pony, he reached out his hand and stroked his neck.

The panic that Lucky had felt since he had met the man with the sour smell melted away. The boy held onto a piece of Lucky's mane and clucked with his tongue. Up until then he had made no sound, and Lucky sensed that there was something different about this silent boy. Something different, but not something to fear.

The boy led the pony out of the river, holding onto his mane but never tugging or pulling. When they were back on the shore, the dog

danced around Lucky, barking. The boy pushed
the dog away gently. Then he crouched down
and examined the slashes on Lucky's legs.
He gasped.

The edges of the cuts gaped open, swollen
and red. Lucky bunched his muscles, ready to
jerk back in pain, but the boy just looked and
didn't touch. Lucky blew out his breath through
his nostrils.

The boy stood up and brushed the hair off
his forehead while he thought about what to do.
Then he made a clucking sound again and started
to walk along the bank, the dog scampering
beside him. He looked back and smiled when he
saw that Lucky was following them. He led the
pony around a bend in the river, walking slowly
and matching his steps to Lucky's painful ones.
He stopped several times so Lucky could rest.

They walked past four small brown cabins
tucked back in the trees. At the end of the row of
cabins, beside a meadow, nestled a bigger house,

painted moss green with yellow trim. It had a wide front porch that faced the river.

A golden retriever and a black and white spaniel, tails wagging, ran out to meet the boy. A goat tethered on a line looked up, grass hanging from his mouth. A stripey orange cat watched from the porch railing, his ears twitching.

A man and a woman were sitting on the porch. The man had gray hair tied back in a ponytail and was wearing bib overalls. He was reading a book. The woman, dressed in faded jeans and a blue shirt, was shelling peas into a wooden bowl. They both stood up as the boy approached.

The boy led Lucky right up to the porch. The pony planted his feet, his head hanging, refusing to take another burning step.

"We have to help him," said the boy.

In the four months that the boy had been living with the man and woman, these were the first words he had ever spoken.

CHAPTER FIFTEEN

A week went by and no one phoned about Lucky.

"Go outside and play, Tory," said Cathy. "You're as jumpy as a rabbit."

"She's driving me crazy," complained Julia. "All she talks about is Lucky."

On Thursday morning, Tory went to the general store with Oliver to buy some milk and pick up the mail. She ran to the bulletin board to look at her sign. Her heart sank when she saw that all the little tabs with their phone number were still there.

When they got back to the house, Tory spotted Linda's blue car right away. Sometimes Linda came just to say hello and visit, but this time Tory was sure that Linda was going to tell her about her new foster family. She felt sick to her stomach at the thought of moving into a house full of strangers and starting all over again.

Tory took her time getting out of the car. Julia was coming back from the barn after riding Barnabas. "Your *social worker's* here," she said unpleasantly.

"I *know* that," said Tory.

She slipped in the front door. She wanted to sneak up the stairs to her room, but Cathy called out from the living room, "Come on in here, Tory. Linda's got some news."

The two women were drinking tea. Linda grinned at Tory. "Hi, kiddo," she said.

"Hi," mumbled Tory. She liked Linda. Linda was always cheerful and friendly, and she had a long braid almost to her waist that Tory admired. But today Tory didn't smile back.

"Sit down," said Cathy.

Tory thought Cathy sounded nervous. She perched on the edge of an armchair.

"Linda's found you a new foster home," said Cathy quickly. "You're going to live with Daphne Minter. She owns the bookstore in Springton. I've met her and she's a very nice lady."

Cathy said the words *very nice* in a loud voice. She's feeling guilty, thought Tory. She looked at Linda. "Does she have any pets?"

"She lives in an apartment right in town," said Linda. "She's in that new building. I don't think they allow pets. But there's an indoor swimming pool."

She added softly, "I want you to give it a chance, Tory. Really try to like it there."

A hard lump filled Tory's throat. Sometimes Linda seemed like her friend, but today it felt as if she was a traitor. Tory wouldn't look at her.

"I'm going to take you into town tomorrow to meet Daphne," said Linda. "You can have a visit at the bookstore and then she'd like you to see the apartment and have lunch with her."

"How long will I have to stay?"

"Just an hour or two. Just to get acquainted. That way it won't feel so strange when you move in."

Cathy straightened a stack of magazines that were already tidy. She didn't meet Tory's eyes.

"Can I go to my room now?" whispered Tory.

Tory's feet felt like lead as she climbed the stairs. That night, when she went to bed, she tried hard to get excited about the swimming pool. But she couldn't. And she knew she would hate living in a stuffy little apartment instead of a real house with a yard.

Then she felt a flicker of hope. If Daphne Minter owned a bookstore, she must love books. She would hate the fact that Tory was a terrible reader. She probably would be so disgusted that she wouldn't want to keep her.

ᑌ ᑌ ᑌ

The next morning, Cathy told Tory to take her backpack, with an apple for a snack, and her jacket, because it was going to rain. She had never fussed like that before. Tory wondered if she was feeling a teeny-tiny bit sorry about forcing Tory to go to a new home. She backed away when Cathy for once tried to give her a quick hug.

Linda tried to talk to Tory on the drive into town, but Tory stared out the window and didn't answer her. With a sigh, Linda gave up and turned on the radio.

Some days it seemed to take forever to drive to town, but today the trip flew by. When Linda pulled up in front of the bookstore, Tory felt sick. She wasn't ready. She wanted to be somewhere else – anywhere else.

The store was called Huckleberry Books. It had a big front window full of books with bright covers, and a red door. Tory had walked past the store before, but she had never been inside.

"You'll like it in here," said Linda.

She opened the door and a bell jingled. A woman with short silver hair was lifting books out of a cardboard box on a counter. She smiled. "Hi, Linda! And you must be Tory. Hello, Tory! I'm Daphne."

"Hi," mumbled Tory. Daphne had dangly earrings that were tiny gold books! Tory knew she was staring and pulled her eyes away.

"I'll drop her off at your office at one o'clock," Daphne told Linda.

Linda squeezed Tory's hand. "Have fun," she said, and then she was gone.

Tory studied a rack of bookmarks, pretending to be interested. She was afraid that Daphne was going to ask her a bunch of questions. Her throat felt dry and she didn't think she would be able to talk. But Daphne just said, "Would you like to take off your backpack and leave it with my purse?"

"No," said Tory. She liked wearing her backpack. It made her feel that she could leave at any minute if she wanted to.

"Well then," said Daphne. "I won't be too long, and then we'll shut up the store and go for lunch. Why don't you go and pick out a book to keep? The children's books are on that far wall."

Tory drifted over to the wall. She didn't want a book but she thought Daphne might get mad if she said so. So she found a shelf with chapter books and she pulled them out, one at a time, and pretended to be choosing.

A woman came in and asked about gardening books. Then a man came in looking for a book about training dogs. After that the store was quiet.

"How are you getting along?" called out Daphne.

"Fine," said Tory.

She slid a book off of the shelf and her heart gave a little jump. On the cover was a glossy picture of a black horse. The first word in the title was easy – *Black*. She could guess the second word – *Beauty*. Tory had seen the movie, and she had cried and cried in the sad parts. She loved the pony called Black Beauty almost as much as she loved Lucky. But she hadn't known there was a book. She flipped through the pages. There were no pictures, and the print was small, and the book was thicker than the others she had looked at. But the cover was so beautiful! She took the book up to the front of the store and showed it to Daphne. "I've picked one," she said.

Daphne frowned. "I'd like you to choose something you can read," she said.

Tory's cheeks felt as if they were on fire. Linda must have told Daphne that she was a bad reader. "I want this book," she said in a low voice.

"It's too hard for you," said Daphne firmly.

"But I want it," said Tory.

"I'm planning to help you with your reading, Tory," said Daphne in a softer voice. "You'll just get discouraged with a book that's too difficult. How about one of the Magic Tree House books? Or the Polk Street series? They don't have so many words. And I've got some great picture books."

Picture books! Did Daphne think she was a *baby*? Did she think she was *stupid*? What exactly had Linda told her? Heat rose up Tory's neck. Before she could stop herself, she kicked out at the stand of bookmarks. It teetered and then toppled over with a crash.

Tory gasped and her heart pounded. She waited for Daphne to yell at her. She took a big breath, so she would be ready to yell back. She was ready to tell Daphne that she didn't want her help, and she *didn't* want to live with her.

Daphne sighed. "Put the book back, Tory. You can pick one some other day." She sounded a little cold, but she didn't scream or anything.

Her legs shaking, Tory took the book back to the children's section. She looked longingly at the cover. Then she glanced over at Daphne, who was kneeling on the floor, picking up bookmarks.

Tory slipped the book into her backpack.

CHAPTER SIXTEEN

Tory was instantly sorry that she had taken the book – sorry and frightened. She had never stolen anything before. But it was too late to put it back. Daphne was right beside her, telling her it was time to go.

They walked to Daphne's apartment building, which was only a few blocks away. The whole way, Tory felt hot with shame about the book in her backpack.

Everything about the apartment building

looked new – the row of skinny trees along the walkway, the gleaming black-and-white tile floor in the entrance, the rows of shiny mailboxes. They took an elevator to the third floor, the top floor.

When Daphne opened the apartment door, she let Tory go in first. Tory glanced around. The living room was small and there were shelves crammed with books on every wall. "Where's the TV?" she asked.

"I don't watch TV," said Daphne. "So I don't have one."

Tory was shocked. "Do you have a computer?"

"I use the computer at the store. I really don't want two."

No TV! No computer! Tory felt panicky. What was she going to do every day?

Daphne told her to leave her backpack by the front door. She gave her a quick tour of the kitchen and bathroom. She pointed to a closed door. "My bedroom's in there." She opened the door beside it. "And this is your room."

The room was small. It had a bright pink bedspread on the bed, a pink carpet, and pink curtains. In one corner was a dollhouse, almost as tall as Tory.

"What do you think?" said Daphne.

"It's okay, I guess. "

"Well," said Daphne, sounding disappointed. Tory hunched her shoulders. She wasn't going to pretend she liked pink. She hated pink.

"Why don't you play with the dollhouse while I make us some grilled cheese sandwiches?" said Daphne.

Tory didn't like playing with dolls and she had no idea what to do with a dollhouse. Instead, she stood by the window and looked out at the back alley. She watched a thin striped cat nosing around a pile of old boxes beside a dumpster. The cat was like her. It didn't have a home. Nobody loved it. Tory wished she could scoop it up and bring it inside, but there was that stupid rule about no pets.

She was glad when it was time to eat. She had refused breakfast and now she was hungry. Grilled cheese sandwiches were one of her favorite things.

"Well, at least I got something right," said Daphne, watching her gobble up the sandwich. That made Tory feel guilty but she hardened her heart. Why should she care about this woman's feelings?

Daphne glanced at her watch. "We're going to have to eat and run. It's almost one. I'll just throw these dishes in the sink. Do you want to use the bathroom?"

The soap in the bathroom was pale purple and shaped like a shell. There was a bottle of coconut hand cream. Tory rubbed cream on her hands, and on her arms too, because it smelled so good.

When she came out of the bathroom, Daphne was standing beside the door, waiting for her. Tory froze. In Daphne's hand was the book *Black Beauty*.

Tory stared at her backpack, which was open at Daphne's feet.

"It's started to rain," said Daphne. "I was looking to see if you had a jacket."

Tory's legs felt like jelly. She swallowed.

"Oh, Tory," sighed Daphne. She put the book on a table. "I'll take it back to the store later. Linda will be waiting. We should get going."

It would have been better if Daphne had screamed at her. Then Tory could have screamed back that Daphne had no right to snoop in her backpack.

This way, she wanted to curl up in a ball and die.

CHAPTER SEVENTEEN

When they got to Linda's office, Daphne didn't say anything about Tory stealing the book. But Tory knew she would as soon as she got a chance. It made Tory feel awful. She wanted Linda to like her, but she wouldn't after she heard about this. Who would like a thief?

On the way back to Cathy and Oliver's, Tory pretended to be asleep. Linda didn't have time to come in, but she said she would see Tory soon. Tory mumbled, "Good-bye," and walked to the house, her feet dragging.

When Tory opened the door, the phone was ringing in the den. She heard Oliver pick it up and then, after a few seconds, say, "Really! All that way!"

Her heart jumped.

She raced into the den and stood beside Oliver, almost afraid to breathe, as he said things like, "How extraordinary.... His name is Lucky.... It was because of the fire...Well, we are grateful." Oliver gave her a thumbs-up.

In the long pauses while the person on the other end was talking, Tory thought she was going to explode. "Is he okay? Is he *okay*?" she screeched in Oliver's ear.

Oliver frowned at her to be quiet. He listened for a few more minutes and said, "Yes, I know how to find your place. Tomorrow afternoon, then. And thank you again."

Cathy was standing in the doorway, listening too. Oliver hung up. "You'll never believe this!"

he told them. "Lucky went right over the mountain. He showed up at a place called Rainbow Ranch. I remember it from when I was a kid. Hippies used to live there."

"Hippies!" said Cathy.

"That was forty years ago. It sounds like there's just a couple and a child living there now." He grinned. "I was talking to a woman called Summer. Her husband's name is Jonah. I'll bet they wear love beads and bell-bottom pants!"

Tory wasn't sure what hippies were, but she didn't care. "Is Lucky okay?" she demanded.

"He wasn't at first," said Oliver. "Their boy found him. Patrick. He's eleven and he's a foster child like you, Tory. Summer said Lucky's legs were badly cut, probably from barbed wire. But he's getting better quickly. They sound like people who care a lot about animals."

"How did they know to call us?" said Cathy.

"They went into Springton today to sell vegetables at the farmer's market. They stopped at the feed store to pick up some grain and spotted one of Tory's signs on the bulletin board."

"Thank goodness," said Cathy. "Good for you, Tory, for thinking of making signs! Now maybe we'll have some peace around here."

"Can we go right now? Please, *please*!" said Tory.

"Tomorrow." Oliver was using his no-non-sense voice.

Tory sighed. Tomorrow! How could she ever wait that long?

U U U

The next day, Oliver hooked up the horse trailer. Tory sat on the edge of the truck seat all the way to Rainbow Ranch. They had to drive halfway to Springton and then over the mountain before they turned off on a gravel road that Tory had never been on before. The road followed a river that Oliver said was called Rainbow River.

While he drove, he told Tory more about

hippies. "They lived together and grew their own food and played guitars and the men all had long hair. They didn't have proper jobs. They said things like *groovy* and *far out*."

"And they wore love beads and bell-bottom pants," she reminded him.

"Right."

Tory thought it must have been a lot of fun to be a hippie. She especially loved the peace sign that Oliver showed her how to make with her fingers. She leaned out the window and flashed the sign at some cows in a field.

When they arrived at Rainbow Ranch, a little gray dog, a black and white spaniel, and a golden retriever all rushed out to greet them. Summer was thinning carrots in a large vegetable garden beside the house. She stood up and waved and walked over to the truck. Tory was disappointed. Summer was wearing ordinary blue jeans and a plaid shirt. There was no sign of any love beads! But she had a friendly smile.

"I hope you don't mind dogs," she said. This is Monty, Charlie, and Emma. They can be a bit wild, but not one of them would hurt a flea."

"I love dogs!" Tory laughed when Monty, the golden retriever, put his front paws on her chest.

"Down, Monty," said Summer, but she didn't sound cross. "Jonah's out in his workshop. I'll tell him you're here and then I hope you've got time for some iced tea and cookies."

"I'll take you up on that," said Oliver, "but I think Tory here will burst if she doesn't see old Lucky."

"He's in the barn with Patrick," said Summer. "The wire cuts have mostly healed. Patrick's looked after him all by himself. He's been marvelous. He's put ointment and new bandages on every day."

Tory could hear the pride in Summer's voice. No one ever sounded like that when they talked about *her*. "Can I go see Lucky now?"

A shadow passed over Summer's face. "Of

course, but, oh my, this is going to be hard for Patrick." She hesitated. "I wasn't going to tell you, but I think I should. Patrick came to live with us four months ago. He didn't talk, not one word."

Tory was shocked. Oliver had said Patrick was eleven. What kind of eleven-year-old didn't talk? "Why?" she asked.

"Patrick has been through a very bad time. But he's healing, like Lucky." Summer's face broke into a smile. "That's when Patrick started to talk to us, when he found your pony. I think Lucky opened up a door inside him that had been shut tight. And he's been talking more and more."

"That's wonderful," said Oliver. "It's hard work being a foster parent."

"We're getting another foster child tomorrow," said Summer. "We wouldn't right now except it's an emergency. Her name is Hilary. Her current foster home can't keep her."

Tory fidgeted.

"Off you go, Tory," said Summer.

She pointed out the way and Tory raced to the barn.

CHAPTER EIGHTEEN

Lucky was standing in a stall, in a deep bed of clean straw. His front legs were wrapped in bandages right up to his knees. There was no sign of Patrick.

"Lucky!" cried Tory. Her throat closed up and tears burned behind her eyes. She opened the stall door and flung her arms around Lucky's shaggy neck. The pony's ears flickered back and forth and he nickered softly.

Tory knelt down and inspected Lucky's legs. The bandages were clean and white.

She was impressed by how neatly and snugly they were wrapped. Summer was right – that boy, Patrick, had done a good job.

Lucky nuzzled the back of Tory's neck. She grinned, stood up and gave the pony another huge hug. "You're going home today," she told him. "You're going home, Lucky."

Something stirred inside Tory – a little voice that reminded her. It was Lucky's home. Not hers. She only had two more weeks and then she would be gone. Cathy had said that if she didn't move too far away, she could come sometimes on the weekends and ride Lucky. But Tory knew it wouldn't be the same. Besides, Cathy would probably forget that she had ever promised that.

She blinked hard. *I won't think about that right now*, she thought. *I won't!* Something in the corner of the stall caught her eye. The straw was pressed down, as if someone spent a lot of time sitting there, and there was a book with a bookmark in it. Tory wouldn't have been interested except for the picture of a black horse on the cover.

She stared in disbelief. It was *Black Beauty!* The book was much older than the one in the store, and the cover wasn't shiny. She picked it up and opened it to the first page. It was a jumble of words she couldn't read. Just for a second, she wished she were a better reader. Then she told herself, fiercely, *I don't care!*

"What are you doing with my book?" said a cold voice.

Tory looked up. A boy stood in the doorway of the stall, holding a handful of carrots that were still covered in dirt from the garden. He had brown tousled hair, a pale white face, and blazing dark eyes. His eyes were swollen and rimmed with red, as if he had been crying for a long time.

Patrick.

She dropped the book into the straw. She stared back at him, her heart thumping.

He stepped into the stall. "What are you doing here?" he said.

She swallowed. "I've come for Lucky."

"You can't have him." His voice was low, like a whisper, and Tory thought she had heard wrong.

"What?"

"You can't have him. He's mine."

"No he's not!" said Tory.

Two red spots appeared in Patrick's cheeks. "I found him! I looked after him! He would have been dead if it wasn't for me. You didn't care about the fire. You didn't care what happened to him. You just left him to die!"

Tory's mouth dropped open. It wasn't true. It was Oliver who had abandoned Lucky, not her. Anger flared inside her.

"How dare you!" she shouted. "How dare you say that! You don't know. You weren't there!"

"Go!" said Patrick. "Now! I mean it! Get out of here! Just go!"

He raised his arm and Tory thought he was

going to fling the carrots at her. Or maybe even hit her. "*Go!*"

She sucked in her breath. Oliver would know what to do.

She marched past Patrick, out of the stall.

"I'll be back!" she said.

CHAPTER NINETEEN

Oliver was sitting on the porch with Summer and Jonah.

"Oliver—" began Tory.

He frowned. "You're interrupting."

Summer smiled. "Go inside the house and get yourself a juice box, Tory. Then bring it out here and you can have some cookies."

The house was very messy. In the living room there were newspapers scattered on the couch, a rubber bone and ball on the floor, mugs on the coffee table, and a pile of knitting in an armchair. Tory spotted the orange cat asleep on the windowsill, and she stroked his head carefully.

She found the kitchen, got a juice box out of the fridge, and headed back through the living room. But she paused in the doorway to the porch.

Cathy had once told her that it was a very bad habit of hers, standing in doorways and listening to people's conversations. She said it was sneaky. But Tory knew that when adults lowered their voices, they were often talking about her. And sometimes that was the only way she could find out what was happening.

She held her breath so they wouldn't hear her. But this time, the adults weren't talking about her. They were talking about Lucky.

"How would you feel if we left Lucky at your place?" Oliver asked.

Tory felt as if she had been slammed in the chest. She squeezed her hands into fists.

"From what you tell me, he's made such a difference to Patrick," Oliver went on. "I think it's marvelous how Lucky has helped the boy talk again. They've obviously formed a bond. And we really have no need for the pony. My daughter, Julia, outgrew him years ago."

An icicle slid down Tory's back. Me. *What about me?* she thought.

"I don't know," said Summer slowly.

"It would be a better home for him," said Oliver. "We could consider it a loan. He's neglected at our place. We have enough work with the show horses. To be honest, we don't want Lucky."

"Tory does," said Jonah.

Oliver sighed. "Tory does," he agreed, "but she's leaving, so it really doesn't matter. And you say you have a little girl coming here tomorrow. She might like to have a pony too."

"Well," said Summer, "even so, we wouldn't want Tory to be upset."

"Yes," said Jonah. "We'd feel better about it if Tory agrees."

Tory clenched her fists. Never, *never*, would she agree to leave Lucky with that horrible Patrick.

She ran through the living room and out of the house.

∪ ∪ ∪

She raced down a path that led along the river. As she ran, Oliver's words pounded in her head. *We don't want Lucky. We don't want Lucky.* How could Oliver be so cruel?

She passed some old cabins. Then she spotted something bright and colorful tucked into the trees. She went closer for a better look. It was an old bus, decorated with painted flowers and peace signs. A hippie bus, she guessed.

She opened the door and peered inside. It was empty except for a plaid sleeping bag spread out on the floor. Some books and a drawing pad and a box of pencil crayons were scattered about.

Patrick must come here, she thought. She hesitated and then climbed inside. Patrick was in the barn with Lucky. She could hide here. Far away from Oliver, who wanted to give her pony away. Far away from Summer and Jonah, who wanted her to say that was okay.

If they took Lucky away, would Patrick stop talking again? She swallowed hard.

She tried to imagine something so terrible happening to her that it made her not want to talk. She couldn't imagine anything that bad. But why was she thinking about this? She didn't care about Patrick. She *didn't* care.

She sat down on the sleeping bag. She glanced at Patrick's books but they had boring covers, and they were thick and probably very hard to read. She opened the drawing pad and gave a little gasp.

Patrick had drawn Lucky, standing in a field

of green grass with a blue river behind him. It was a perfect picture. He had drawn Lucky's big dark eyes and shaggy mane just right. She couldn't take her eyes off the picture. Lucky looked so happy, as if he belonged.

After a long time, she heard Oliver's voice in the distance, calling her. Then the bus door opened and Summer's tanned face peered in. "Here you are."

"How did you find me?" asked Tory.

"Patrick always comes here when he wants to think." Summer smiled. "And also it was a lucky guess."

Summer sat down on the sleeping bag beside her. Tory's head was filled with a jumble of thoughts. *We don't want Lucky*, Oliver had said. But Patrick wanted him. He loved Lucky. Tory swallowed. If Patrick stopped talking again, it would be her fault.

She took a deep breath.

"I think Lucky should stay here," she said.

∪ ∪ ∪

Oliver was proud of Tory. He told her so over and over again on the way home.

"That was a hard thing to do, but it was the right thing," he said.

Tory stared out the window and wished he would stop talking.

When it was time to go, Summer and Jonah had hugged her good-bye. Patrick had muttered, "Thank you," in a gruff voice.

And then they had left and it had been too late for Tory to change her mind. All the way back, she tried to make herself feel better by thinking about how Lucky had found a new home with a family that really wanted him.

She blinked back tears.

What was going to happen to her?

CHAPTER TWENTY

The next day, at lunch, Cathy said, "Linda called while you were playing outside. She thinks it would be a good idea to get you settled before school starts. You're going to Daphne at the end of the week, on Friday. By then, all the paper-work will be finished."

Friday!

"I thought I was staying two more weeks," said Tory weakly. She had been so sure that Daphne wouldn't want her anymore, and that

Linda would have to look for another home. She pushed away her peanut butter sandwich. She would be sick if she ate another bite.

For the next two days, everyone was extra nice to Tory – even Julia, who let her listen to her iPod and play her best computer games. Oliver took her out on the ATV, and Cathy made pancakes with strawberries and whipped cream for breakfast.

"This isn't really good-bye," said Cathy, when Linda came to get Tory on Friday. "You'll come back to visit us."

Yeah, right, thought Tory. Cathy and Oliver and Julia would forget all about her by tomorrow. She stared straight ahead as she and Linda drove out the driveway. She was positive that by now Daphne would have told Linda about her stealing *Black Beauty*. She braced herself.

But Linda just said, "Did I tell you I'm taking you out for a hamburger and a milkshake and anything else you want?" Then she put some music on the radio and didn't say anything else.

Tory leaned back against the seat. This was weird. Usually Linda chatted nonstop, trying to get her to talk about her feelings.

∪ ∪ ∪

"I have to talk to you about something," said Linda.

When someone said that, it always meant something bad was coming. Was it about stealing the book? Was it about the way she got mad at people? Tory scraped up the last scoop of ice-cream sundae and let it slide down her throat. She stared at Linda.

"Last week, I arranged for a girl called Hilary to live with the family at Rainbow Ranch." Linda glanced at the café door and then away again.

"I know," said Tory. "I've been to Rainbow Ranch. That's where Lucky is."

"Yes, Cathy told me." Linda leaned across the table. "It hasn't worked out for Hilary."

"It hasn't?"

Those were the words Cathy used when she talked about Tory. *It hasn't worked out. We want our little family back.*

"Didn't they like her?" said Tory.

"Oh yes, they did," said Linda. "But it turns out that Hilary's terribly allergic to cats and dogs. She's never been around them much before, so no one knew. By yesterday, she couldn't stop sneezing and she could hardly breathe. So I brought Daphne out to the ranch last night to meet her."

"Hilary is going to live with Daphne too?" said Tory slowly. She tried to imagine sharing that yucky pink bedroom with another girl.

"She's there now. Hilary is a real bookworm, just like Daphne. I think they'll get on fine."

Linda sighed, but it didn't sound like a real sigh. It sounded like a pretend sigh. "Now we have a great big problem. Daphne has room for only one foster child."

"And she'd rather have Hilary," whispered

Tory. "She hates me. She thinks I'm stupid." To her surprise, she felt a little bit jealous of Hilary. The apartment was awful, but Daphne was sort of nice and she had kept Tory's secret about the book.

"She doesn't hate you at all," said Linda, looking surprised. "Why on earth would you think that? She told me you had spunk. And she wants you to come back to the bookstore and visit. But I told Daphne that I'd had second thoughts that an apartment might not be the best place for you. I think that you would be much happier if you could have a pet."

Tory went still inside. "Summer said Hilary was an emergency. Am I an emergency now?"

"Not an emergency." Linda grinned. "But you are the girl that Jonah and Summer really want. Right away." Linda looked up at the door again, and this time she waved.

Tory spun around. Summer walked into the café, wearing a long patchwork skirt and something around her ankle that looked like love beads. Behind her came Jonah, and then Patrick. Summer and Jonah smiled at Tory. Patrick's face was red and he stared at the floor in front of his feet.

Summer said, "Patrick?"

Patrick raised his eyes. He took a step toward Tory. "I'm sorry I shouted at you," he said. "I was just so…upset. But I didn't mean the things I said."

"That's okay," whispered Tory. She shouted at people too, when she got upset. She knew what it felt like.

"I wanted to keep Lucky so much. He helped me." Patrick looked right at her. "It's really hard to talk about. Some day I'll explain."

"You don't have to," said Tory.

"Anyway, I really want you to live at Rainbow Ranch." Patrick's words poured out now. "Lucky wants you to come too. We could hang out together. And I could even help you with your reading. If you want."

Tory sucked in her breath.

Patrick's face split into a wide grin. "So, will you come?"

Tory thought he would make a pretty neat brother. Jonah and Summer were nice, and she could play with the orange cat and all those dogs. Best of all she would see Lucky every single day.

Tory grinned back. "You bet I will!"

U U U

Tory rode Lucky along a trail beside the river. A cool September breeze ruffled her hair. The air was crisp and it seemed ages since the terrible days of the forest fire.

Last week, Oliver had phoned and said that Lucky could stay at Rainbow Ranch forever. Tory and Patrick were sharing him, and Jonah said he would look for another pony to keep Lucky company.

Jonah had put shoes on Lucky and his hooves made a clopping sound. Tory rode past the cabins and all the way to a dead tree that leaned over the water. This was the place where Jonah and Summer said she should turn around. She tipped forward and patted Lucky's neck. Her head whirled with plans.

That morning, she had baked a pan of chocolate brownies all by herself. Summer had helped her read the recipe, and had given her some neat tricks for sounding out hard words. They had a deal. Tory could cook anything she wanted, as long as she read the recipe herself, with Summer's help.

In the afternoon, Tory and Patrick were going to eat brownies in the old hippie bus. Patrick was reading *Black Beauty* to her and she couldn't wait for the next chapter.

A bright yellow leaf twirled down from a tree and landed like a butterfly on the ground. In the distance, she heard Charlie, the spaniel, barking. She remembered that she had promised to help Patrick brush burrs and mats out of all the dogs' coats today. She clucked to Lucky and squeezed her legs on his sides to get him moving.

For once, Lucky didn't mind trotting. He knew that the two of them were on the way home.

ACKNOWLEDGMENTS

I would like thank everyone at Second Story Press who worked so hard on this story, particularly my editor, Gena Gorrell, whose insight and ideas were invaluable.

I would like to thank my good friend Helen Helvoight who answered my many questions about social workers and foster children. Thanks also to my writing pals, Ainslie, Kathy, and Ann, who listened to the early drafts and, as always, were encouraging, supportive, and so much fun!

ABOUT THE AUTHOR

BECKY CITRA is a former teacher and the author of seventeen books for children. She lives on a ranch in Bridge Lake, British Columbia where she loves to ride horses, hike, snowshoe, and cross-country ski. She brings her knowledge of the outdoors into her books, often writing about ranch life and the wilderness.